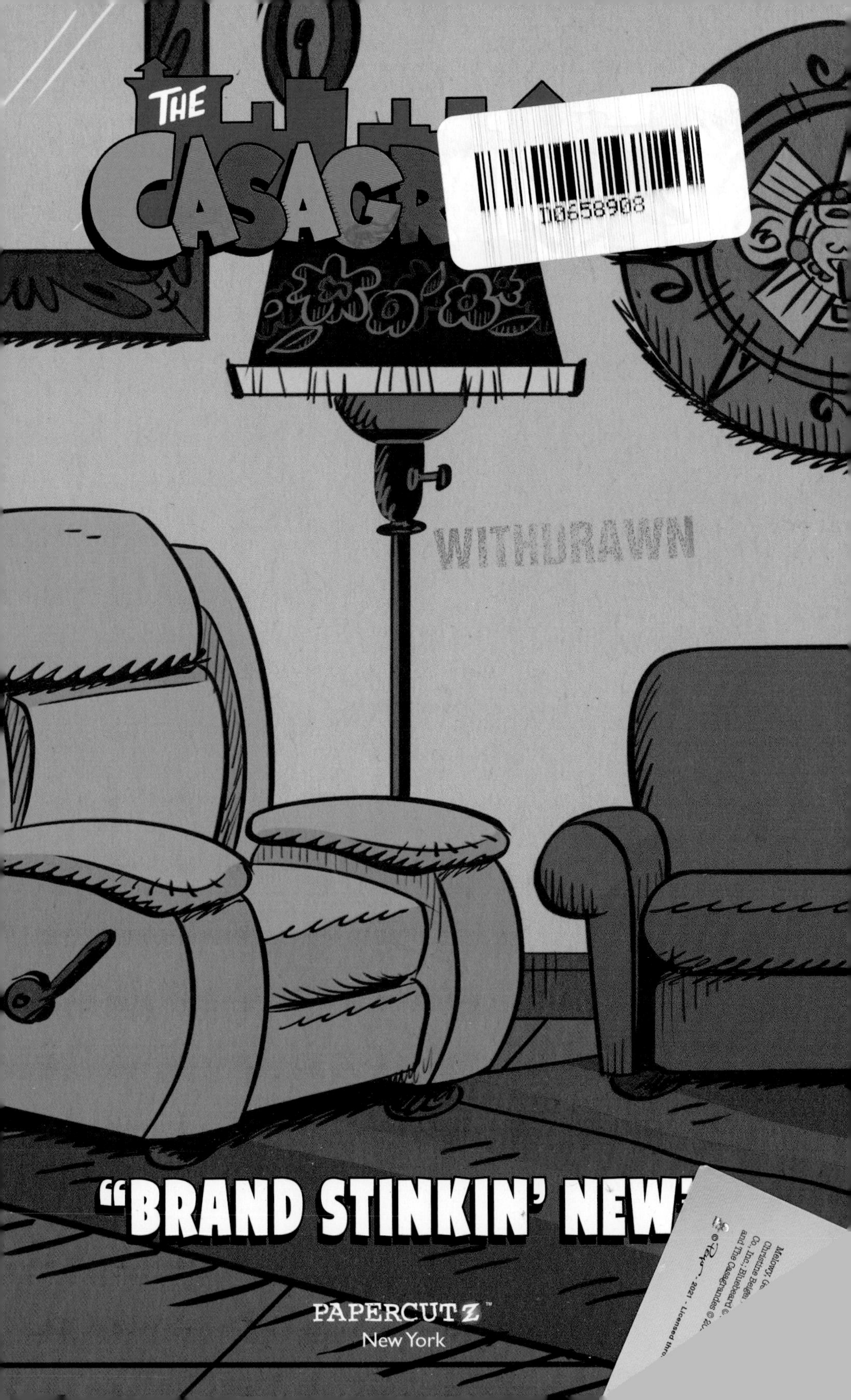

THE CASAGR

"BRAND STINKIN' NEW"

PAPERCUTZ™
New York

MORE GREAT GRAPHIC NOVEL SERIES AVAILABLE FROM
PAPERCUTZ™

THE SMURFS TALES

BRINA THE CAT

CAT & CAT

THE SISTERS

ATTACK OF THE STUFF

LOLA'S SUPER CLUB

SCHOOL FOR EXTRATERRESTRIAL GIRLS

GERONIMO STILTON REPORTER

THE MYTHICS

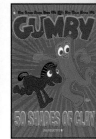

GUMBY

MELOWY

BLUEBEARD

GILLBERT

ASTERIX

FUZZY BASEBALL

THE CASAGRANDES

THE LOUD HOUSE

ASTRO MOUSE AND LIGHT BULB

GEEKY F@B 5

THE ONLY LIVING GIRL

papercutz.com
Also available where ebooks are sold.

THE CASAGRANDES

#3 "BRAND STINKIN' NEW"

"CUT AND RUN"
Derek Fridolfs — Writer
Amanda Tran — Artist, Colorist
Wilson Ramos Jr. — Letterer

"CHEER UP"
Paloma Uribe — Writer
Kelsey Wooley — Artist, Colorist
Wilson Ramos Jr. — Letterer

"LALO FOREVER"
Paloma Uribe — Writer
Zazo Aguiar — Artist, Colorist
Wilson Ramos Jr. — Letterer

"OLD SOLE"
Amanda Fein — Writer
Zazo Aguiar — Artist, Colorist
Wilson Ramos Jr. — Letterer

"SICKBED RIVALRY"
Kacey Huang-Wooley — Writer
D.K. Terrell — Artist, Colorist
Wilson Ramos Jr. — Letterer

"PRANKS FOR NOTHING"
Derek Fridolfs — Writer
Lex Hobson — Artist, Colorist
Wilson Ramos Jr. — Letterer

"FUSION FOR A BRUISIN'"
Caitlyn Connelly — Writer
Jennifer Hernandez — Artist, Colorist
Wilson Ramos Jr. — Letterer

"CASA TO THE MOON"
Paloma Uribe — Writer
Zazo Aguiar — Artist, Colorist
Wilson Ramos Jr. — Letterer

"LEAVE A MESSAGE AT THE BAWK!"
Amanda Fein — Writer
Zazo Aguiar — Artist, Colorist
Wilson Ramos Jr. — Letterer

"A SUPER HARRRD CHOICE"
Derek Fridolfs — Writer
Izzy Boyce Blanchard — Artist
Erin Rodriguez — Colorist
Wilson Ramos Jr. — Letterer

"LATE AGAIN"
Paloma Uribe — Writer
Zazo Aguiar — Artist, Colorist
Wilson Ramos Jr. — Letterer

"A TIE GAME"
Derek Fridolfs — Writer
Daniela Rodriguez — Artist, Colorist
Wilson Ramos Jr. — Letterer

"TRASH OR TREASURE"
Caitlyn Connelly — Writer
Lex Hobson — Artist, Colorist
Wilson Ramos Jr. — Letterer

"SERGIO'S BIG BREAK"
Paloma Uribe — Writer
Zazo Aguiar — Artist, Colorist
Wilson Ramos Jr. — Letterer

"A BLANKET STATEMENT"
Derek Fridolfs — Writer
Amanda Tran — Artist, Colorist
Wilson Ramos Jr. — Letterer

"LIMITED EDITION"
Jair Holguin — Writer
Amanda Lioi — Artist
Lex Hobson — Colorist
Wilson Ramos Jr. — Letterer

AMANDA TRAN — Cover Artist

Preview "SLEEPLESS IN PRESCHOOL" Kara Fein — Writer; Amanda Lioi — Artist, Colorist; Wilson Ramos Jr. — Letterer

JAMES SALERNO — Sr. Art Director/Nickelodeon

JAYJAY JACKSON — Design

KRISTEN G. SMITH, DANA CLUVERIUS, MOLLIE FREILICH, NEIL WADE, MIGUEL PUGA, LALO ALCARAZ,
JOAN HILTY, KRISTEN YU-UM, EMILIE CRUZ, and ARTHUR "DJ" DESIN — Special Thanks

KARLO ANTUNES — Editor

STEPHANIE BROOKS — Assistant Managing Editor

JEFF WHITMAN — Comics Editor/Nickelodeon

MICOL HIATT — Comics Designer/Nickelodeon

JIM SALICRUP
Editor-in-Chief

ISBN: 978-1-5458-0911-2 paperback edition
ISBN: 978-1-5458-0910-5 hardcover edition

Papercutz books may be purchased for business or promotional use. For information on bulk purchases please contact Macmillan Corporate and Premium Sales Department at (800) 221-7945 x5442.

Printed in India
May 2022

Distributed by Macmillan
First Printing

THE CASAGRANDES

Theme Song Performed by: ALLY BROOKE
Theme Song Composed by: GERMAINE FRANCO
Lyrics by: GERMAINE FRANCO, MIKE RUBINER & LALO ALCARAZ
Rap Lyrics Performed by: IZABELLA ALVAREZ

I'm in the big city with my big familia [family]

Everyday here is my favorite día [day]

One big house and our family store
Food and laughter ¡y mucho amor! [and a lot of love!]

Tíos [aunts and uncles], abuelos [grandparents], all of my primos [cousins]...

A dog, a parrot, amigos! [friends!]

We're one big family now!
Sundays and Mondays
They're all fun days when you're with the...
Casagrandes!
¡Mucha vida! [A lot of life!]

Casagrandes!
¡Bienvenida! [Welcome!]

Casagrandes!
¡Mucha risa! [A lot of laughs!]

Casagrandes!
We're all familia! [Family!]

¡Tan-tan! [Tah-dah!]

MEET THE CASAGRANDES
and friends!

RONNIE ANNE SANTIAGO

Ronnie Anne's a skateboarding city girl now. She's fearless, free-spirited, and always quick to come up with a plan. She's one tough cookie, but she also has a sweet side. Ronnie Anne loves helping her family, and that's taught her to help others too. When she's not pitching in at the family *mercado*, you can find her exploring the neighborhood with her best friend Sid, or ordering hot dogs with her skater buds Casey, Nikki, and Sameer. Having a family as big as the Casagrandes has taught Ronnie Anne to deal with anything life throws her way.

BOBBY SANTIAGO

Bobby is Ronnie Anne's big bro. He's a student and one of the hardest workers in the city. He loves his family and loves working at the *mercado*. As his *abuelo's* right hand man, Bobby can't wait to take over the family business one day. He's a big kid at heart, and his clumsiness gets him into some sticky situations at work, like locking himself in the freezer. Mercado mishaps aside, everyone in the neighborhood loves to come to the store and talk to Bobby.

MARIA CASAGRANDE SANTIA

Maria is Bobby and Ronnie Anne's mom. As a nurse at the city hospital, she's hardworking and even harder to gross out. For years, Maria, Bobby, and Ronnie Anne were used to only having each other… but now that they've moved in with their Casagrande relatives, they're embracing big family life. Maria is the voice of reason in the household and known for her always-on-the-go attitude. Her long work hours means she doesn't always get to spend time with Bobby and Ronnie Anne; but when she does, she makes that time count.

HECTOR CASAGRANDE

Hector is Carlos and Maria's dad, and the *abuelo* of the family (that means grandpa)! He owns the *mercado* on the ground floor of their apartment building and takes great pride in his work, his family, and being the unofficial "mayor" of the block. He loves to tell stories, share his ideas, and gossip (even though he won't admit it). You can find him working in the *mercado*, playing guitar, or watching his favorite *telenovela*.

ROSA CASAGRANDE

Rosa is Carlos and Maria's mom and the *abuela* of the family (that means grandma)! She's the head of the household, the wisest Casagrande, and the master cook with a superhuman ability to tell when anyone in the house is hungry. She often tries to fix problems or illnesses with traditional Mexican home remedies and potions. She's very protective of her family… sometimes a little too much.

CARLOS CASAGRANDE

Carlos is Maria's brother. He's married to Frida, and together they have four kids: Carlota, C.J., Carl, and Carlitos. Carlos is a Professor of Cultural Studies at a local college. Usually he has his head in the clouds or his nose in a textbook. Relatively easygoing, Carlos is a loving father and an enthusiastic teacher who tries to get his kids interested in their Mexican heritage.

FRIDA PUGA CASAGRANDE

Frida is Carlota, C.J., Carl, and Carlitos' mom. She's an art professor and a performance artist, and is always looking for new ways to express herself. She's got a big heart and isn't shy about her emotions. Frida tends to cry when she's sad, happy, angry, or any other emotion you can think of. She's always up for fun, is passionate about her art, and loves her family more than anything.

CARLOTA CASAGRANDE

Carlota is CJ, Carl, and Carlitos' older sister. A social media influencer, she's excited to be like a big sister to Ronnie Anne. She's a force to be reckoned with, and is always trying to share her distinctive vintage style tips with Ronnie Anne.

CJ (CARLOS JR.) CASAGRANDE

CJ is Carlota's younger brother and Carl and Carlitos' older brother. He was born with Down Syndrome. He lights up any room with his infectious smile and is always ready to play. He's obsessed with pirates and is BFFs with Bobby. He likes to wear a bowtie to any family occasion, and you can always catch him laughing or helping his *abuela*.

CARL CASAGRANDE

Carl is wise beyond his years. He's confident, outgoing, and puts a lot of time and effort into looking good. He likes to think of himself as a suave businessman and doesn't like to get caught playing with his action figures or wearing his footie PJs. Even though Bobby is nothing but nice to him, Carl sees his big cousin as his biggest rival.

CARLITOS CASAGRANDE

Carlitos is the baby of the family, and is always copying the behavior of everyone in the household—even if they aren't human. He's a playful and silly baby who loves to play with the family pets.

LALO

Lalo is a slobbery bull mastiff who thinks he's a lapdog. He's not the smartest pup, and gets scared easily… but he loves his family and loves to cuddle.

SERGIO

Sergio is the Casagrandes' beloved pet parrot. He's a blunt, sassy bird who "thinks" he's full of wisdom and always has something to say. The Casagrandes have to keep a close eye on their credit card as Sergio is addicted to online shopping and is always asking the family to buy him some new gadget he saw on TV. Sergio is most loyal to Rosa and serves as her wing-man, partner-in-crime, taste-tester, and confidant. Sergio is quite popular in the neighborhood and is always up for a good time. When he's not working part time at the *mercado* (aka messing with Bobby), he can be found hanging with his roommate Ronnie Anne, partying with Sancho and his other pigeon pals, or trying to get his ex-girlfriend, Priscilla (an ostrich at the zoo), to respond to him.

SID CHANG

Sid is Ronnie Anne's quirky best friend. She's new to the city but dives headfirst into everything she finds interesting. She and her family just moved into the apartment one floor above the Casagrandes. In fact, Sid's bedroom is right above Ronnie Anne's. A dream come true for any BFFs.

CASEY

Casey is a happy-go-lucky kid who's always there to help. He knows all the best spots to get grub in Great Lakes City. When he is not skateboarding with the crew, he loves working with his dad, Alberto, on their Cubano sandwich food truck.

BECKY

A tough as nails classmate of Ronnie Anne and the skater kids. She makes a good match for her girlfriend, Dodge, captain of the Chavez Academy dodgeball team. Becky has a taste for chaos and destruction that she shares with her younger brother, Ricky, and her loyal dog, Malo. In a pinch though, Becky will definitely come through for a friend in need!

NIKKI

Nikki is as daring as she is easygoing and laughs when she is nervous. When she's not hanging with her buds at the skatepark, she likes checking out the newest sneakers and reading books about the paranormal.

LAIRD

Laird is a total team player and the newest member of Ronnie Anne's friends. Despite often being on the wrong end of misfortune, Laird is an awesome skateboarder who can do tons of tricks…unfortunately stopping is not one of them.

SAMEER

Sameer is a goofy sweetheart who wishes he was taller, but what he lacks in height, he makes up for with his impressive hair and sweet skate moves. He is always down for the unexpected adventure and loves entertaining his friends with his spooky tales!

LINCOLN LOUD

Lincoln is Ronnie Anne's dearest friend from Royal Woods. They still keep in touch and visit one another as often as they can. He has learned that surviving the Loud household with ten sisters means staying a step ahead. He's the man with a plan, always coming up with a way to get what he wants or deal with a problem, even if things inevitably go wrong. Lincoln's sisters may drive him crazy, but he loves them and is always willing to help out if they need him.

STANLEY CHANG

Stanley Chang is Sid's dad. He's a conductor on the GLART-train that runs through the city. He's a patient man who likes to do Tai Chi when he gets stressed out. He likes to cheer up train commuters with fun facts, but emotionally he breaks down more than the train does.

ADELAIDE CHANG

Adelaide Chang is Sid's little sister. She's 6 years old, and has a flair for the dramatic. You can always find her trying to make her way into her big sister Sid's adventures.

VITO FILLIPONIO

Vito is one of Rosa and Hector's oldest and dearest friends, and a frequent customer at the Mercado. He's lovable, nosy, and usually overstays his welcome, but there is nothing he wouldn't do for his loved ones and his dogs, Big Tony and Little Sal.

BIG TONY & LITTLE SAL

MS GALIANO

Ms. Galiano is Ronnie Anne and the skater kid's teacher at Cesar Chavez Academy. She is sweet as pie and often relies on the kids to keep her up to date on the new, hip, pop culture trends. She briefly dated Ronnie Anne's dad, Arturo, and even though it didn't work out, they still remain friends.

"CUT AND RUN"

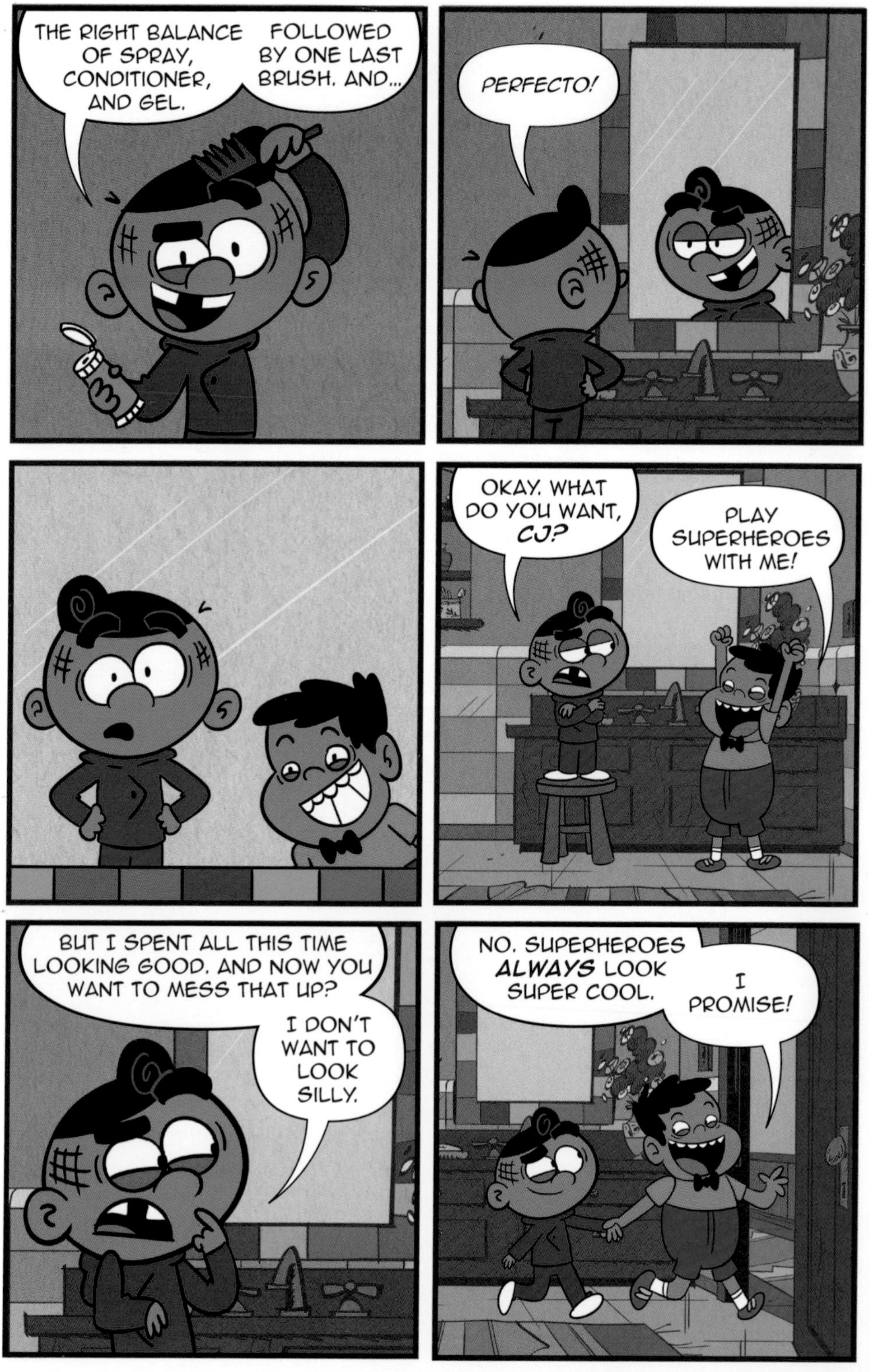
THE RIGHT BALANCE OF SPRAY, CONDITIONER, AND GEL.
FOLLOWED BY ONE LAST BRUSH. AND...
PERFECTO!
OKAY. WHAT DO YOU WANT, CJ?
PLAY SUPERHEROES WITH ME!
BUT I SPENT ALL THIS TIME LOOKING GOOD. AND NOW YOU WANT TO MESS THAT UP?
I DON'T WANT TO LOOK SILLY.
NO. SUPERHEROES ALWAYS LOOK SUPER COOL.
I PROMISE!

"LALO FOREVER"

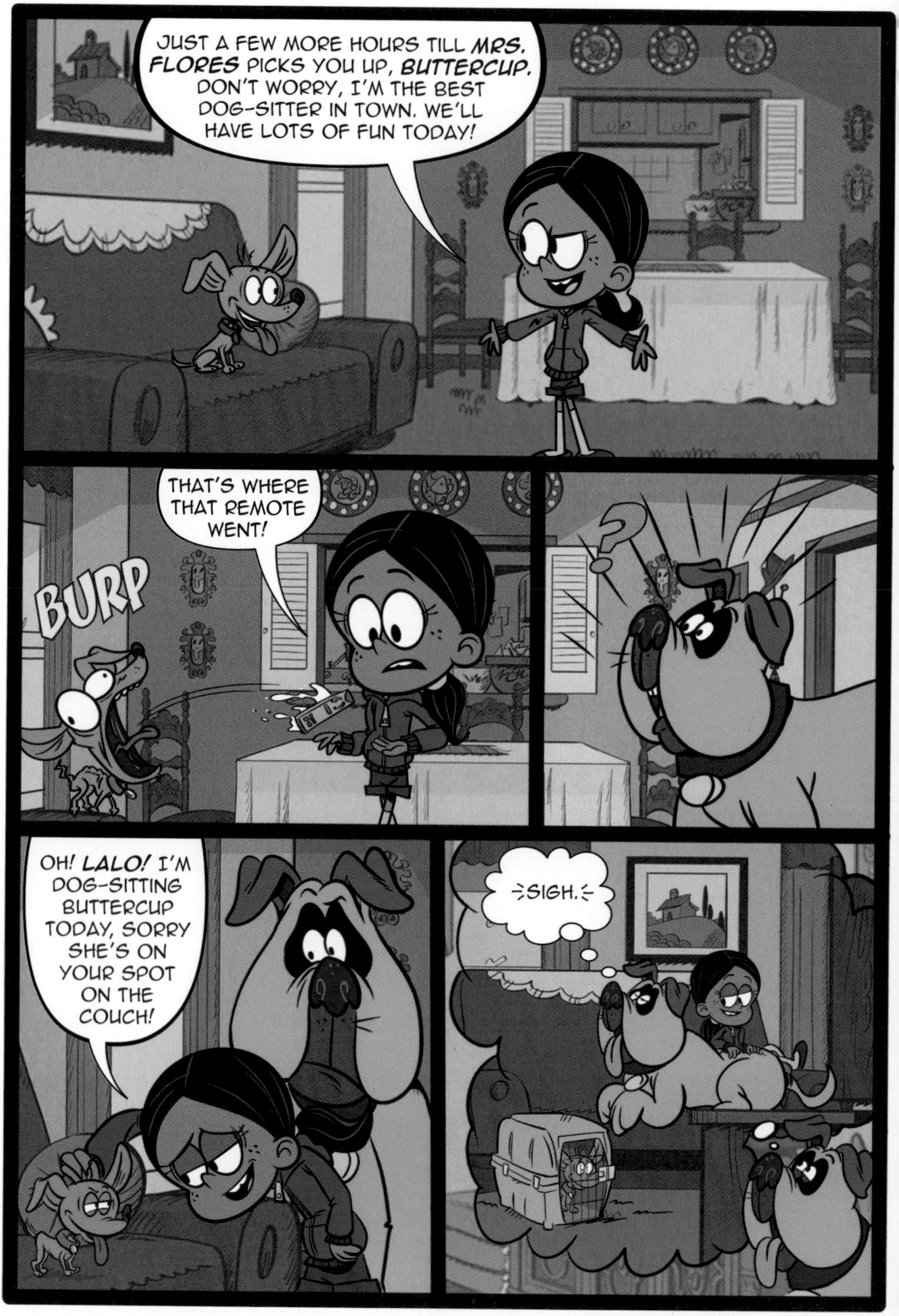
JUST A FEW MORE HOURS TILL MRS. FLORES PICKS YOU UP, BUTTERCUP. DON'T WORRY, I'M THE BEST DOG-SITTER IN TOWN. WE'LL HAVE LOTS OF FUN TODAY!
BURP
THAT'S WHERE THAT REMOTE WENT!
?
OH! LALO! I'M DOG-SITTING BUTTERCUP TODAY, SORRY SHE'S ON YOUR SPOT ON THE COUCH!
SIGH.

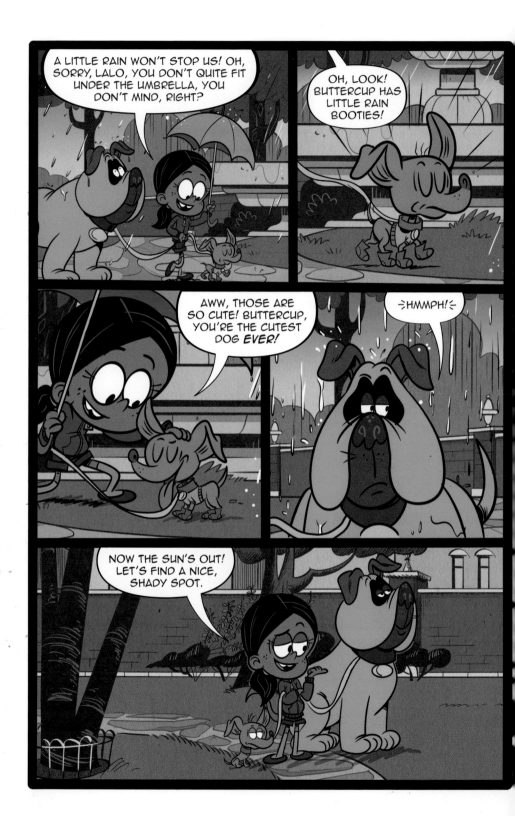

15

"SICKBED RIVALRY"

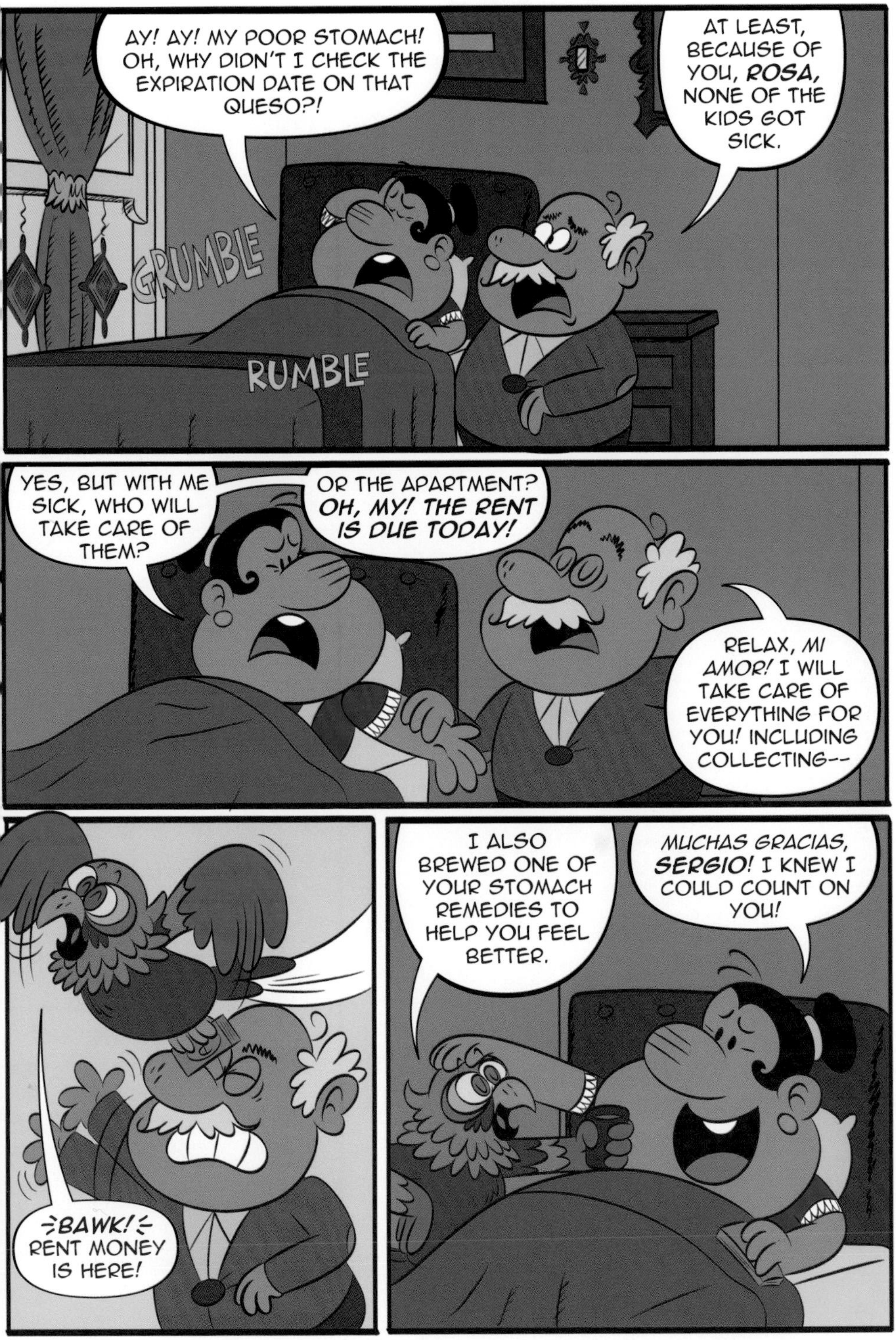

AY! AY! MY POOR STOMACH! OH, WHY DIDN'T I CHECK THE EXPIRATION DATE ON THAT QUESO?!
AT LEAST, BECAUSE OF YOU, ROSA, NONE OF THE KIDS GOT SICK.
GRUMBLE
RUMBLE
YES, BUT WITH ME SICK, WHO WILL TAKE CARE OF THEM?
OR THE APARTMENT? OH, MY! THE RENT IS DUE TODAY!
RELAX, MI AMOR! I WILL TAKE CARE OF EVERYTHING FOR YOU! INCLUDING COLLECTING--
BAWK! RENT MONEY IS HERE!
I ALSO BREWED ONE OF YOUR STOMACH REMEDIES TO HELP YOU FEEL BETTER.
MUCHAS GRACIAS, SERGIO! I KNEW I COULD COUNT ON YOU!

THAT DARN BIRD! I'LL SHOW ROSA WHO SHE CAN REALLY COUNT ON!

THERE! LUNCH FOR THE *FAMILIA* IS DONE!

¡ALMUERZO! WHO WANTS NACHO SOUP?

SORRY, ABUELO, SERGIO ALREADY MADE THIS KILLER FRUIT SALAD!

IT'S DELICIOUS *AND* NUTRITIOUS!

POP

FINE! IF I CAN'T COOK, THEN I'LL JUST TAKE CARE OF THE--

CLEANING?

END

19

"FUSION FOR A BRUISIN"

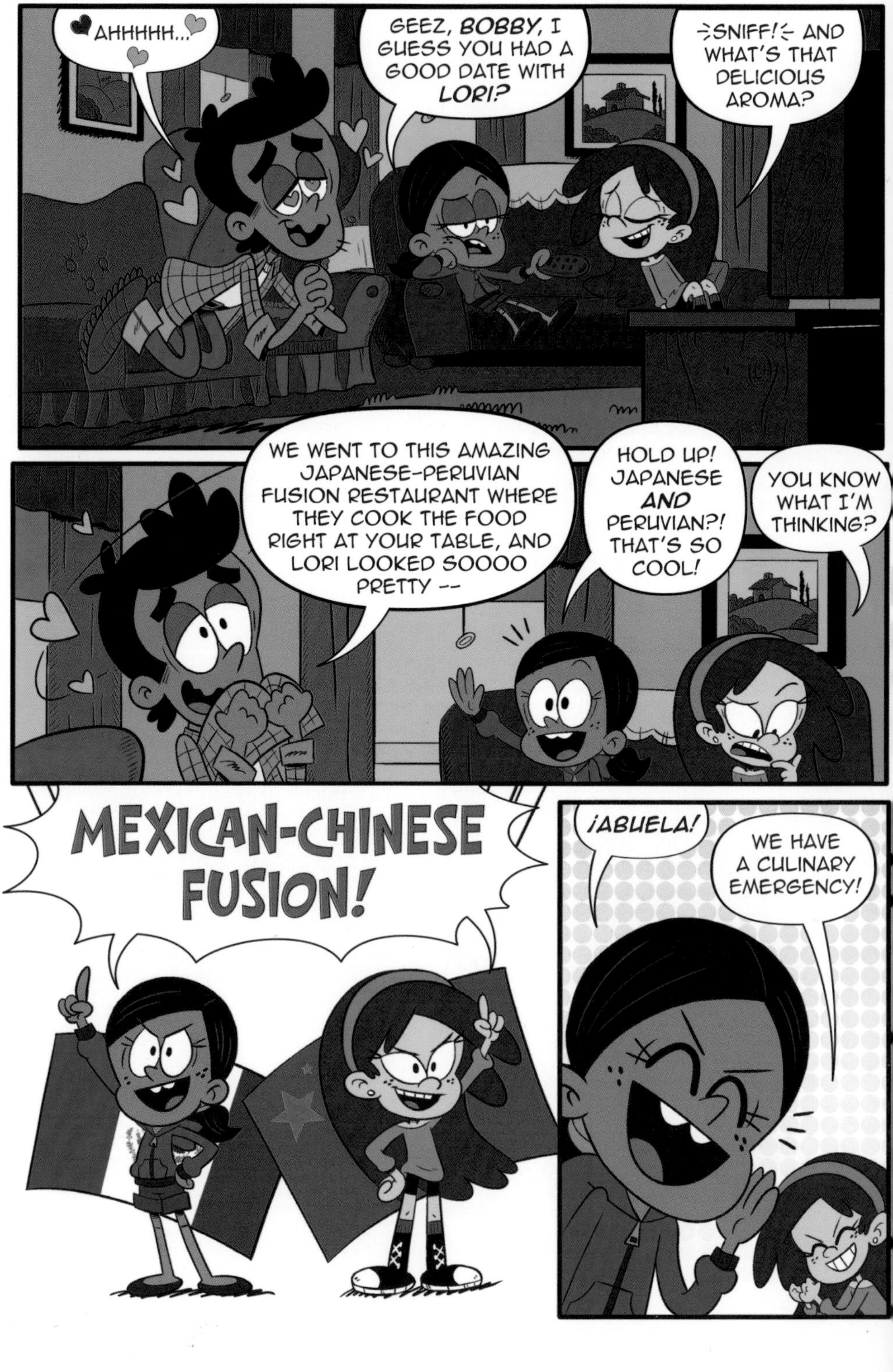
AHHHHH...
GEEZ, BOBBY, I GUESS YOU HAD A GOOD DATE WITH LORI?
SNIFF! AND WHAT'S THAT DELICIOUS AROMA?
WE WENT TO THIS AMAZING JAPANESE-PERUVIAN FUSION RESTAURANT WHERE THEY COOK THE FOOD RIGHT AT YOUR TABLE, AND LORI LOOKED SOOOO PRETTY --
HOLD UP! JAPANESE AND PERUVIAN?! THAT'S SO COOL!
YOU KNOW WHAT I'M THINKING?
MEXICAN-CHINESE FUSION!
¡ABUELA!
WE HAVE A CULINARY EMERGENCY!

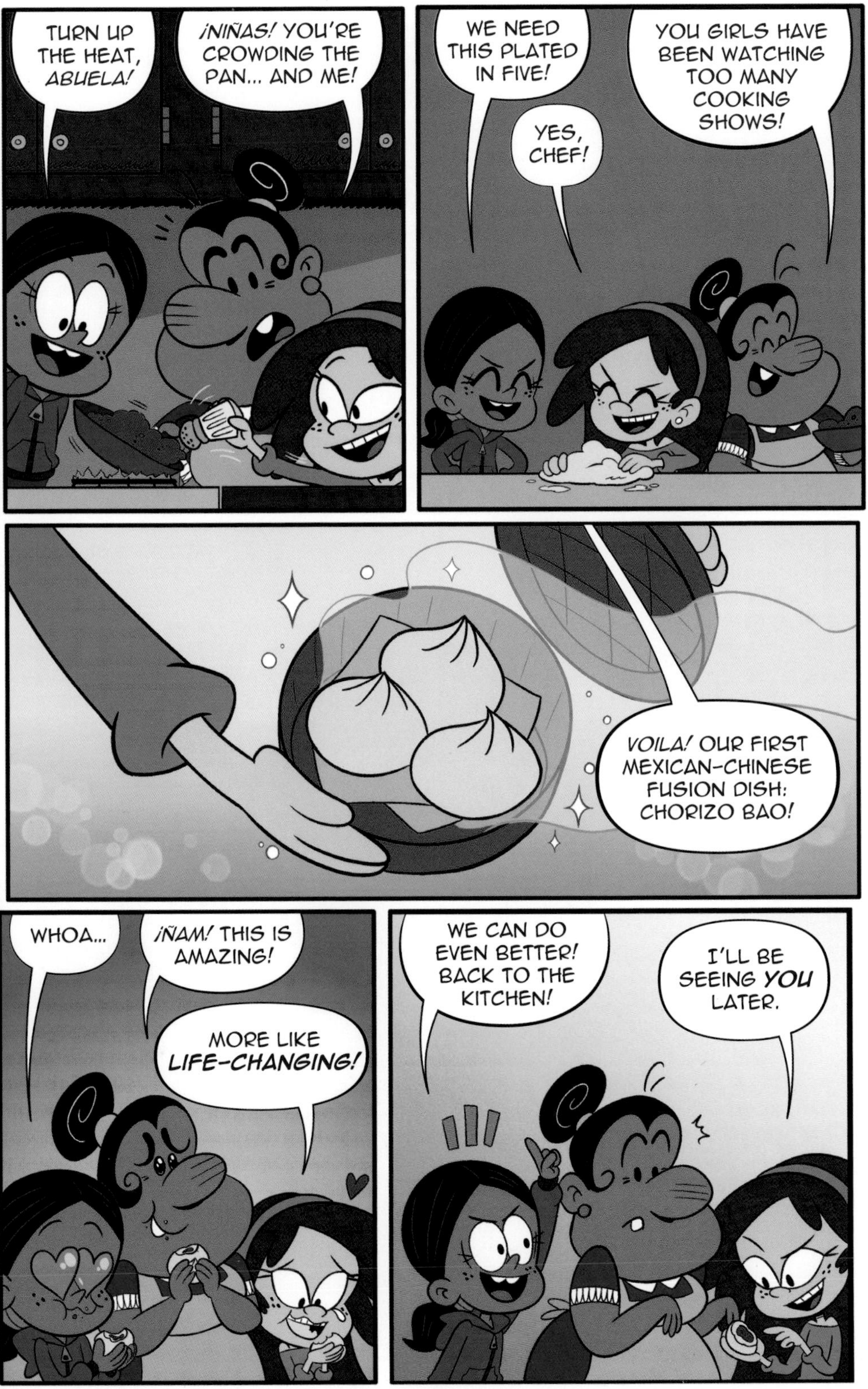
TURN UP THE HEAT, ABUELA!
¡NIÑAS! YOU'RE CROWDING THE PAN... AND ME!
WE NEED THIS PLATED IN FIVE!
YES, CHEF!
YOU GIRLS HAVE BEEN WATCHING TOO MANY COOKING SHOWS!
VOILA! OUR FIRST MEXICAN-CHINESE FUSION DISH: CHORIZO BAO!
WHOA...
¡ÑAM! THIS IS AMAZING!
MORE LIKE LIFE-CHANGING!
WE CAN DO EVEN BETTER! BACK TO THE KITCHEN!
I'LL BE SEEING YOU LATER.

THOSE ONIONS LOOK MORE DICED THAN MINCED!

÷SNIFF!÷

SIZZLE

DAB, FOLD, SQUEEZE!

TAH-DAH! TACO WONTONS, DIM SUM TAMALES, BARBACOA LO MEIN!

¡AY, DIOS MÍO! I'M TIRED, GIRLS!

ALRIGHT, ABUELA, WE'LL TAKE OVER!

WHY SHOULD WE STOP AT MEXICAN-CHINESE FUSION?

WE COULD COMBINE *ANYTHING!*

WE ARE CULINARY *GENIUSES!*

OKAY, MAYBE NOT *GENIUSES...*

"LEAVE A MESSAGE AT THE BAWK!"

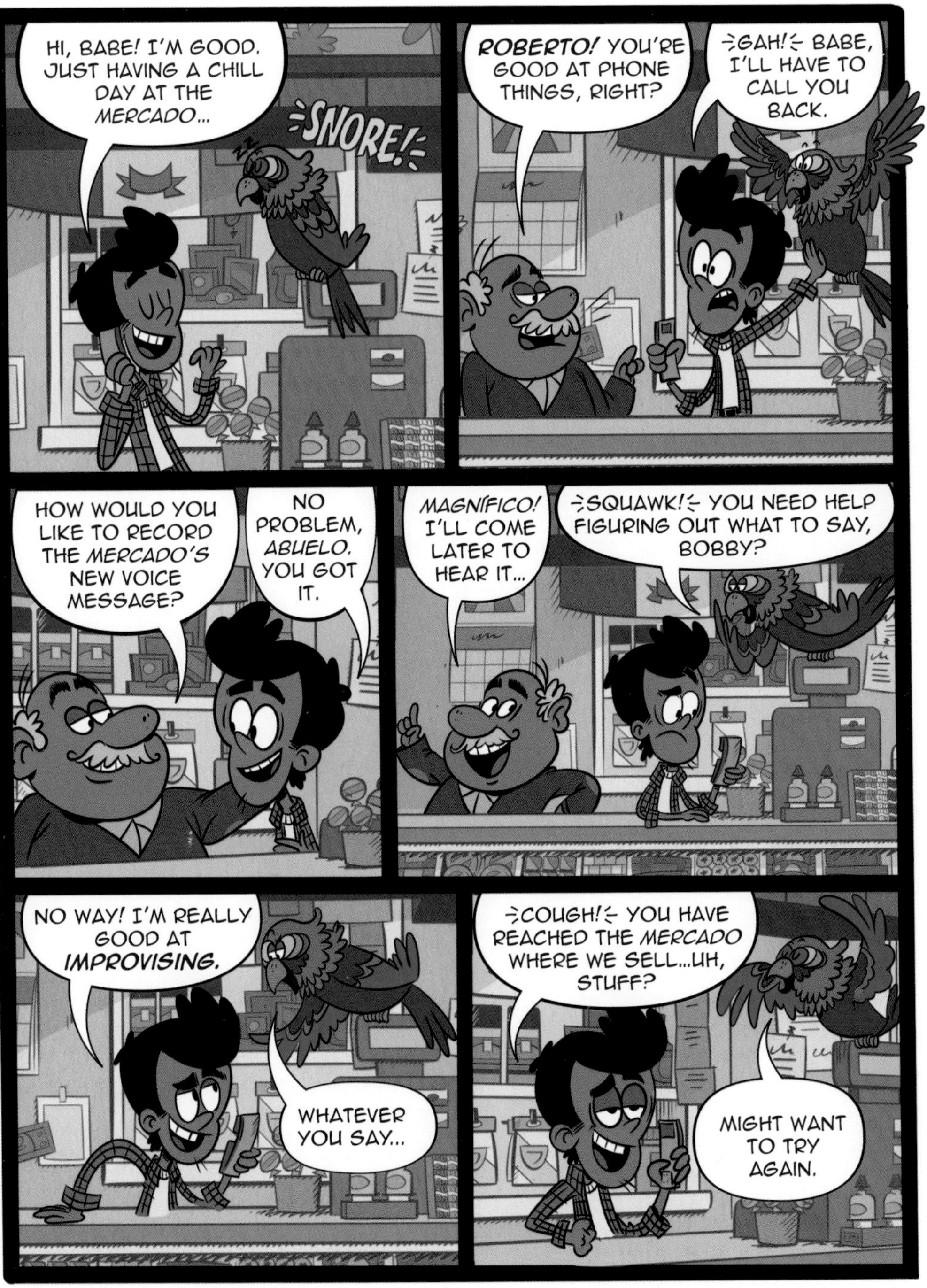
HI, BABE! I'M GOOD. JUST HAVING A CHILL DAY AT THE *MERCADO*...
SNORE!
ROBERTO! YOU'RE GOOD AT PHONE THINGS, RIGHT?
GAH! BABE, I'LL HAVE TO CALL YOU BACK.
HOW WOULD YOU LIKE TO RECORD THE *MERCADO'S* NEW VOICE MESSAGE?
NO PROBLEM, *ABUELO*. YOU GOT IT.
MAGNÍFICO! I'LL COME LATER TO HEAR IT...
SQUAWK! YOU NEED HELP FIGURING OUT WHAT TO SAY, BOBBY?
NO WAY! I'M REALLY GOOD AT *IMPROVISING*.
WHATEVER YOU SAY...
COUGH! YOU HAVE REACHED THE *MERCADO* WHERE WE SELL...UH, STUFF?
MIGHT WANT TO TRY AGAIN.

"LATE AGAIN"

28

"TRASH OR TREASURE"

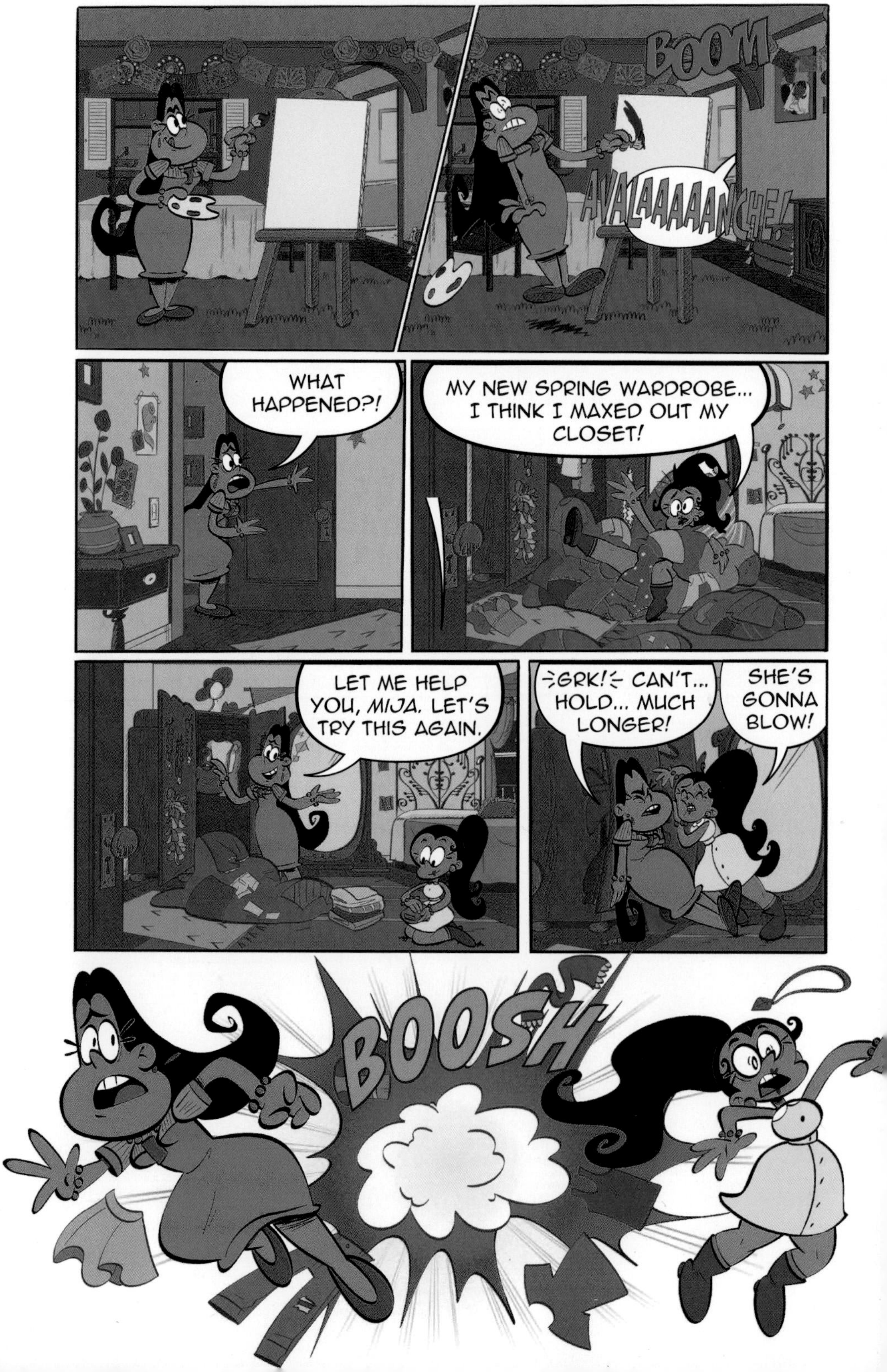
BOOM
AVALAAAAANCHE!
WHAT HAPPENED?!
MY NEW SPRING WARDROBE... I THINK I MAXED OUT MY CLOSET!
LET ME HELP YOU, *MIJA*. LET'S TRY THIS AGAIN.
GRK! CAN'T... HOLD... MUCH LONGER!
SHE'S GONNA BLOW!
BOOSH

"A BLANKET STATEMENT"

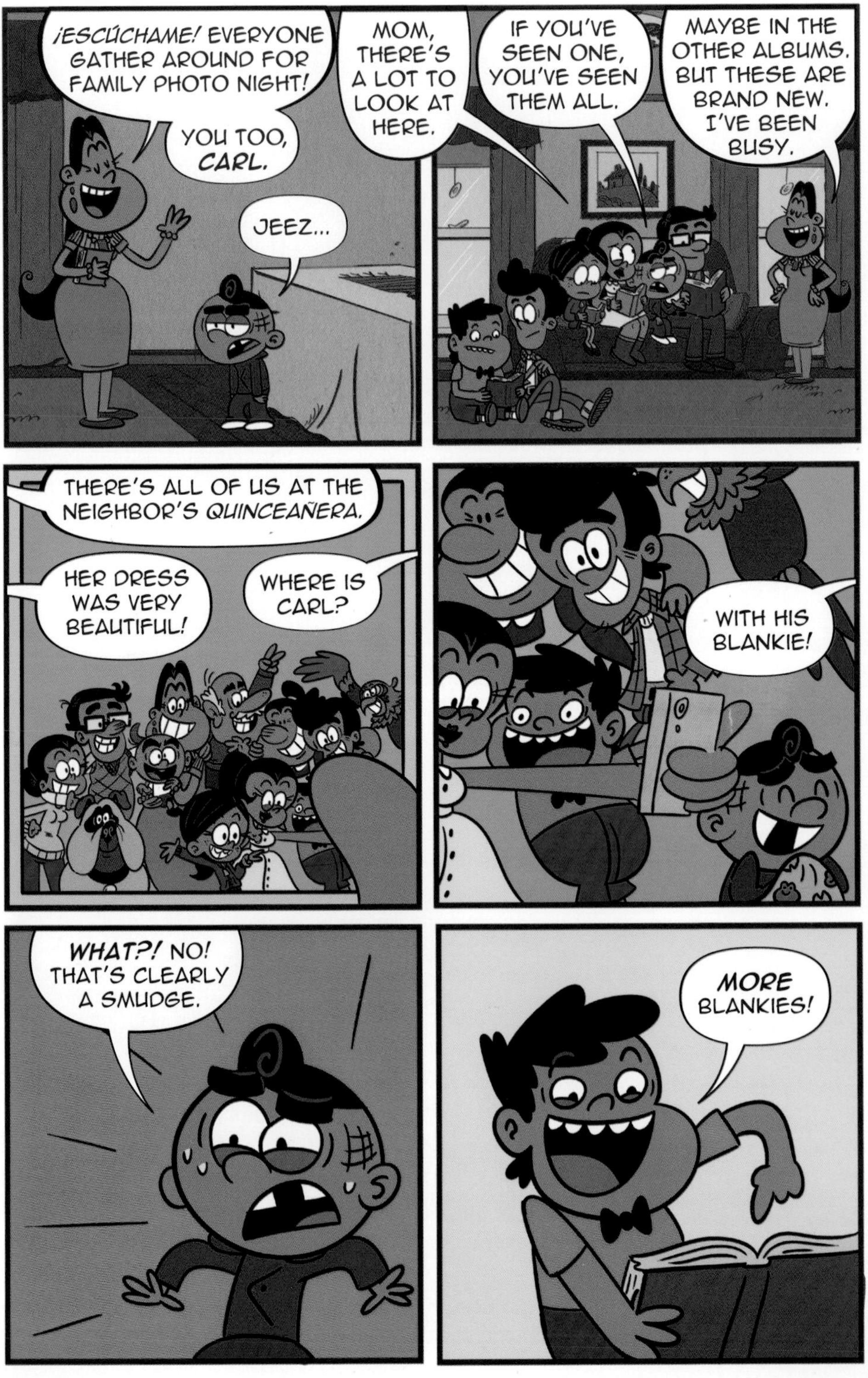

¡ESCÚCHAME! EVERYONE GATHER AROUND FOR FAMILY PHOTO NIGHT!
YOU TOO, CARL.
JEEZ...
MOM, THERE'S A LOT TO LOOK AT HERE.
IF YOU'VE SEEN ONE, YOU'VE SEEN THEM ALL.
MAYBE IN THE OTHER ALBUMS. BUT THESE ARE BRAND NEW. I'VE BEEN BUSY.
THERE'S ALL OF US AT THE NEIGHBOR'S QUINCEAÑERA.
HER DRESS WAS VERY BEAUTIFUL!
WHERE IS CARL?
WITH HIS BLANKIE!
WHAT?! NO! THAT'S CLEARLY A SMUDGE.
MORE BLANKIES!

"CHEER UP"

"OLD SOLE"

43

"PRANKS FOR NOTHING"

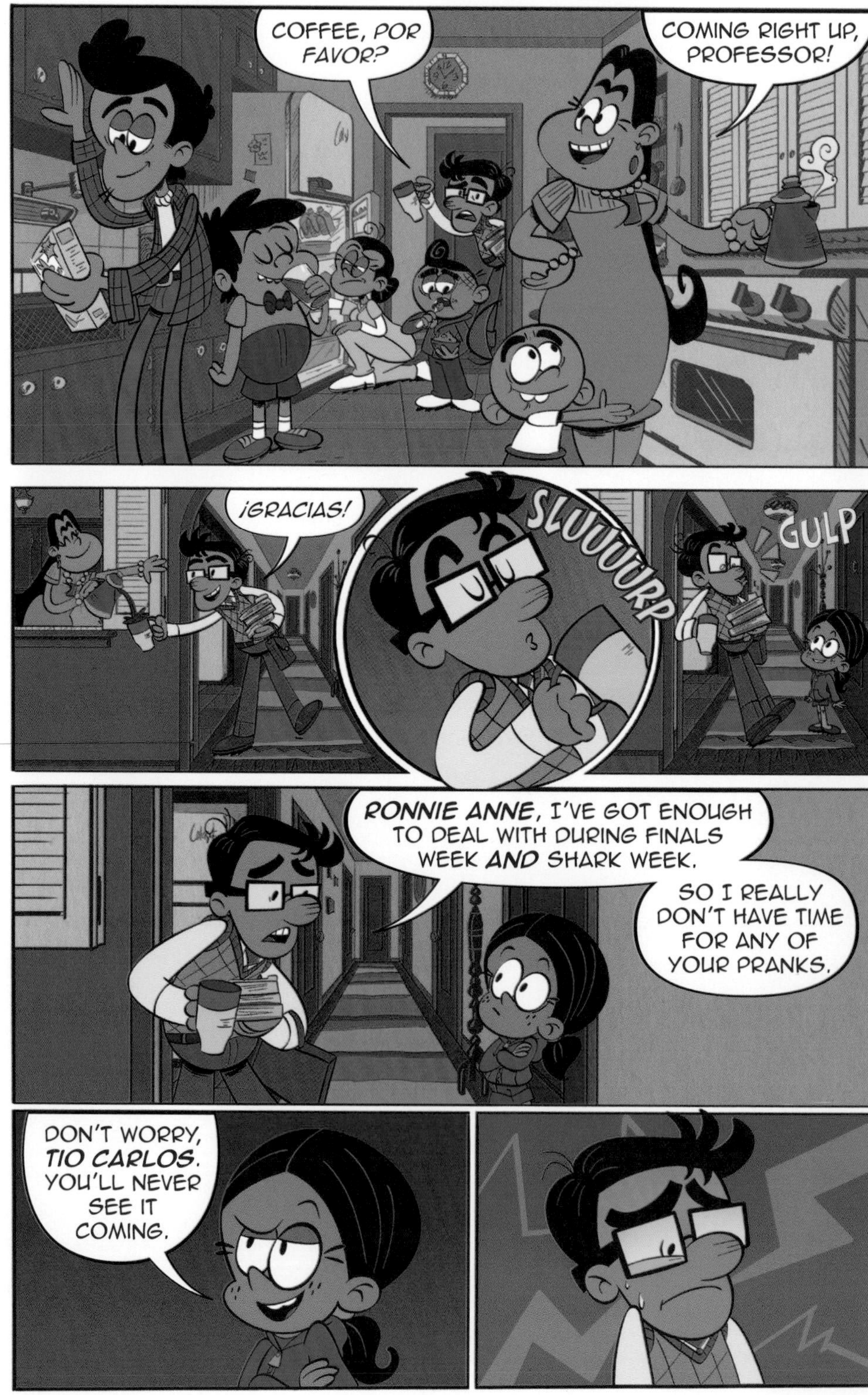

COFFEE, POR FAVOR?
COMING RIGHT UP, PROFESSOR!
¡GRACIAS!
SLUUUURP
GULP
RONNIE ANNE, I'VE GOT ENOUGH TO DEAL WITH DURING FINALS WEEK AND SHARK WEEK.
SO I REALLY DON'T HAVE TIME FOR ANY OF YOUR PRANKS.
DON'T WORRY, TIO CARLOS. YOU'LL NEVER SEE IT COMING.

THE GREAT WHITE SHARK HAS A TREMENDOUS BRAIN IN ADDITION TO BEING AN EFFICIENT HUNTER.

TO BE MORE CLEVER THAN ITS PREY, IT HAS TO HAVE ENOUGH BRAINS TO OUTSMART THEM.

SHE'S LIKE A SHARK STALKING ME IN OPEN WATER!

RING

RING

SAY, UNCLE, I'LL SEE YOU AT HOME.

RONNIE ANNE?!

WHAT'S WRONG? LOST YOUR APPETITE?

RUMBLE

HAVE A NICE DAY, *TIO!*

GOT TO GET TO SCHOOL BEFORE SOMETHING HAPPENS.

TAP. TAP. TAP. TAP

TAP. TAP. TAP. TAP

ALMOST HOME... YEAH.... ALMOST HOME.

CLINK CLANK

OH, IT'S YOU.

RONNIE ANNE! I CAN'T TAKE IT ANYMORE! PLEASE, JUST GET IT OVER WITH! WHAT WAS YOUR PRANK?!

THE PRANK?

OOOOH... THERE WAS NO PRANK. I GUESS THAT'S KIND OF A PRANK IN ITSELF.

IS THAT WHY YOU'RE LATE?

YOU TOTALLY MISSED THE SHARK WEEK PARTY WE THREW FOR YOU.

SORRY YOU MISSED IT. BUT THERE'S ALWAYS NEXT YEAR.

÷SIGH!÷

END

"CASA TO THE MOON!"

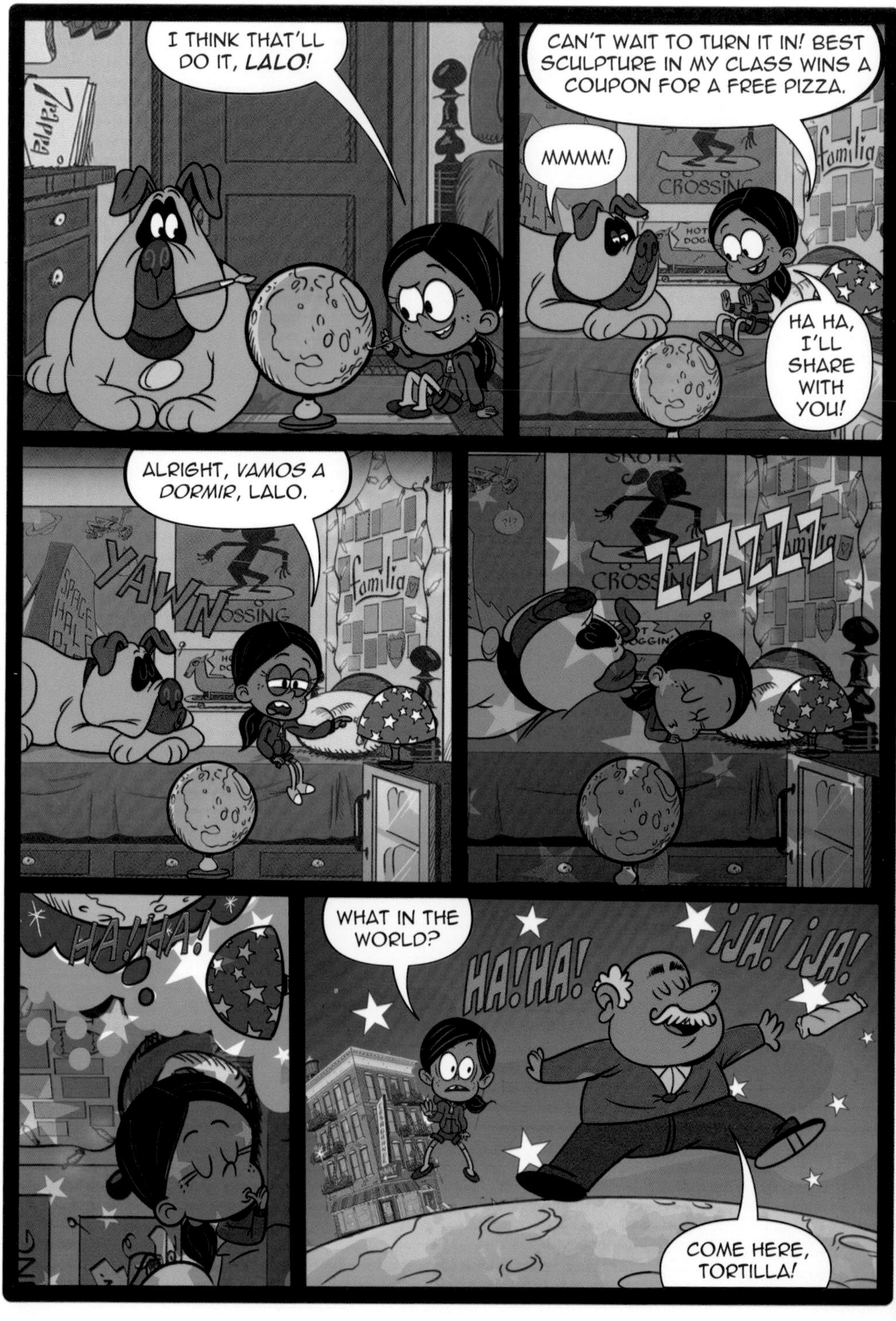
I THINK THAT'LL DO IT, LALO!
CAN'T WAIT TO TURN IT IN! BEST SCULPTURE IN MY CLASS WINS A COUPON FOR A FREE PIZZA.
MMMM!
HA HA, I'LL SHARE WITH YOU!
ALRIGHT, VAMOS A DORMIR, LALO.
YAWN
ZZZZZZ
HA! HA!
WHAT IN THE WORLD?
HA! HA!
¡JA! ¡JA!
COME HERE, TORTILLA!

49

"A SUPER HARRRD CHOICE"

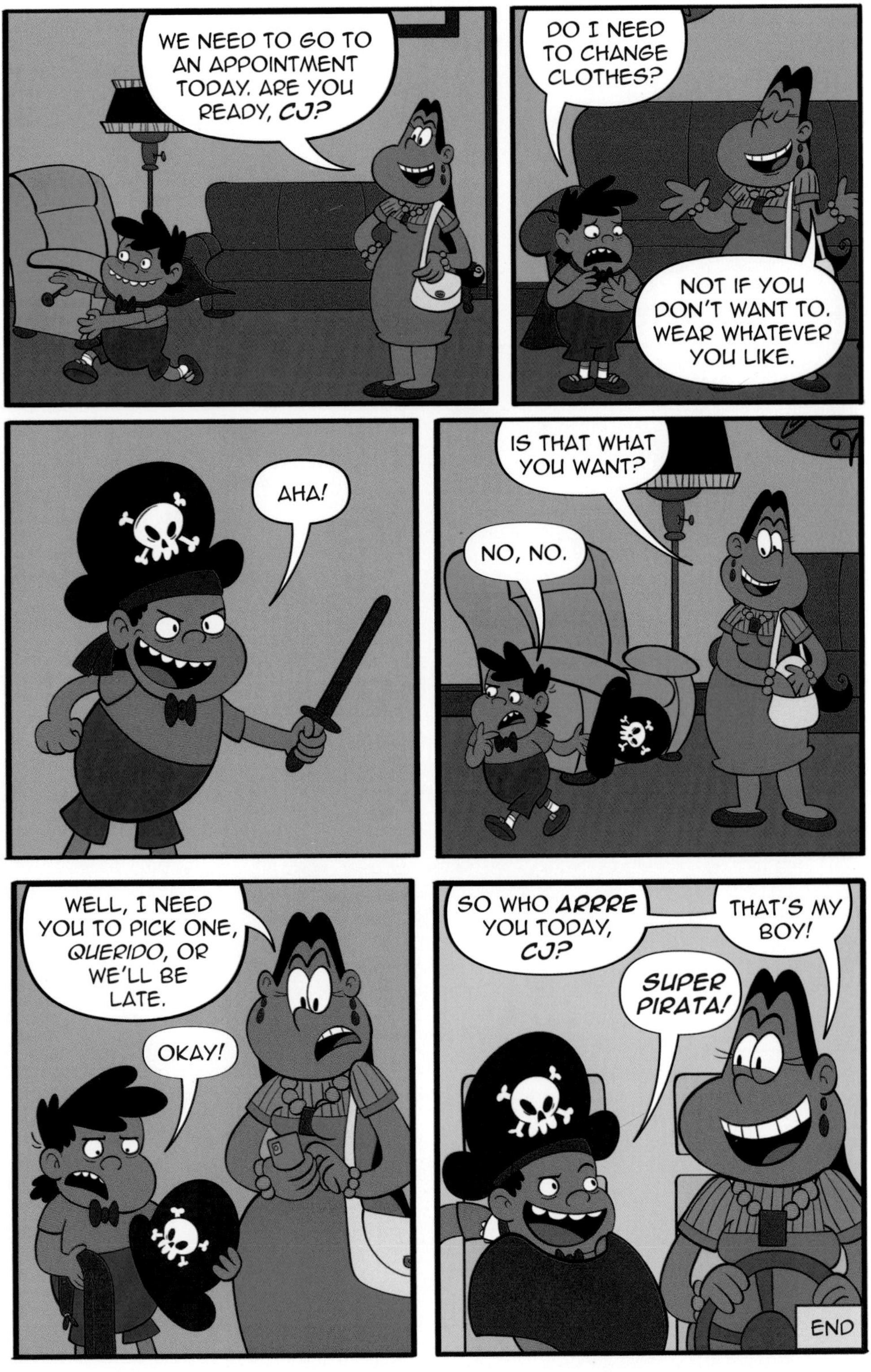
WE NEED TO GO TO AN APPOINTMENT TODAY. ARE YOU READY, *CJ?*
DO I NEED TO CHANGE CLOTHES?
NOT IF YOU DON'T WANT TO. WEAR WHATEVER YOU LIKE.
AHA!
IS THAT WHAT YOU WANT?
NO, NO.
WELL, I NEED YOU TO PICK ONE, *QUERIDO*, OR WE'LL BE LATE.
OKAY!
SO WHO *ARRRE* YOU TODAY, *CJ?*
SUPER PIRATA!
THAT'S MY BOY!
END

"A TIE GAME"

"SERGIO'S BIG BREAK"

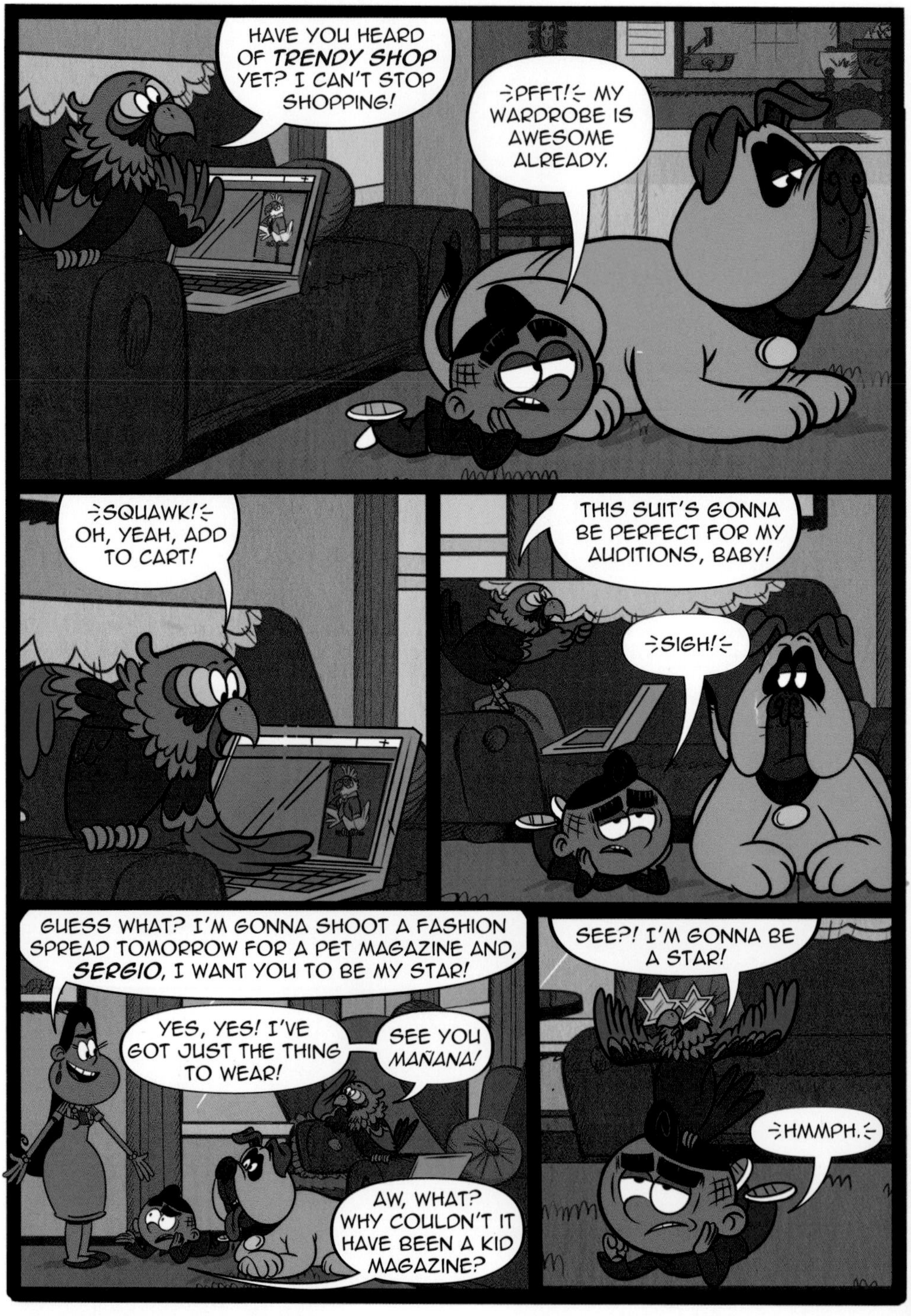
HAVE YOU HEARD OF TRENDY SHOP YET? I CAN'T STOP SHOPPING!
PFFT! MY WARDROBE IS AWESOME ALREADY.
SQUAWK! OH, YEAH, ADD TO CART!
THIS SUIT'S GONNA BE PERFECT FOR MY AUDITIONS, BABY!
SIGH!
GUESS WHAT? I'M GONNA SHOOT A FASHION SPREAD TOMORROW FOR A PET MAGAZINE AND, SERGIO, I WANT YOU TO BE MY STAR!
YES, YES! I'VE GOT JUST THE THING TO WEAR!
SEE YOU MAÑANA!
AW, WHAT? WHY COULDN'T IT HAVE BEEN A KID MAGAZINE?
SEE?! I'M GONNA BE A STAR!
HMMPH.

"LIMITED EDITION"

MAKE WAY FOR THIS SUMMER'S HOTTEST TOY, THE LIMITED EDITION *EL FALCON*! THIS *SLEEK* FIGURE IS ONLY AVAILABLE FOR A LIMITED TIME SO ACT FAST!

WOW!

I HAVE TO ACT FAST. HE EVEN COMES WITH RETRACTABLE FALCON WINGS!

REMEMBER, KIDS, A REAL FALCON FRIEND ALWAYS SHOWS OFF THEIR MERCH WITH *PRIDE*!

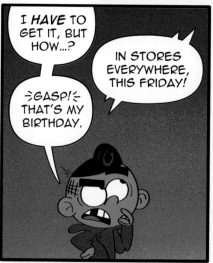

I *HAVE* TO GET IT, BUT HOW...?

IN STORES EVERYWHERE, THIS FRIDAY!

∻GASP!∻ THAT'S MY BIRTHDAY.

HERE YOU GO, *ABUELO*, I GOT THE PAPER FOR YOU!

OH, THANKS, *CARL*, I DIDN'T EVEN KNOW THE PAPER CAME AROUND THIS TIME.

LET'S SEE HERE...

SO, *ABUELO*, MY BIRTHDAY'S COMING UP. I DON'T WANT ANYTHING *TOO* BIG. SOMETHING SMALL LIKE, OH, I DON'T KNOW...

...THE NEW EL FALCON LIMITED EDITION ACTION FIGURE WOULD BE PERFECT.

HMM... THEY REALLY CHANGED THE SPORTS SECTION TODAY.

I BETTER HURRY OR ELSE I'LL MISS THE NEW EPISODE OF --

FELIZ CUMPLEAÑOS!

AHHHH!

HAPPY BIRTHDAY, *QUERIDO!* OPEN THIS ONE FIRST, IT'S FROM ME AND YOUR *ABUELO.*

YOUR *ABUELO* TOLD ME THAT YOU'VE BEEN ASKING FOR THIS ALL WEEK.

I DID? OH, YEAH.

RIIP

HUH?

DO YOU LIKE IT? THEY'RE LIMITED EDITION! AREN'T THEY "SLEEK"?

THIS IS... AWESOME! WOW, EL FALCON CHONIES! THANKS, ABUELA!

YOU KNOW WHAT THEY SAY, A REAL FALCON FRIEND ALWAYS SHOWS OFF HIS MERCH WITH PRIDE!

END

nickelodeon GRAPHIC NOVELS AVAILABLE FROM PAPERCUTZ

nickelodeon
THE LOUD HOUSE
THERE WILL BE CHAOS
PAPERCUTZ

THE LOUD HOUSE
#1
"There Will Be Chaos"

nickelodeon
THE LOUD HOUSE
THERE WILL BE CHAOS

THE LOUD HOUSE
#2
"There Will Be More Chaos"

nickelodeon
THE LOUD HOUSE
LIVE LIFE LOUD!

THE LOUD HOUSE
#3
"Live Life Loud!"

nickelodeon
THE LOUD HOUSE
FAMILY TREE
KEEP OUT!

THE LOUD HOUSE
#4
"Family Tree"

nickelodeon
THE LOUD HOUSE
AFTER DARK

THE LOUD HOUSE
#5
"After Dark"

nickelodeon
HIT SHOW
THE LOUD HOUSE
LOUD & PROUD
PAPERCUTZ

THE LOUD HOUSE
#6
"Loud & Proud"

nickelodeon
THE LOUD HOUSE
THE STRUGGLE IS REAL

THE LOUD HOUSE
#7
"The Struggle is Real"

nickelodeon
THE LOUD HOUSE
LIVIN' LA CASA LOUD!
PAPERCUTZ

THE LOUD HOUSE
#8
"Livin' La Casa Loud!"

nickelodeon
THE LOUD HOUSE
ULTIMATE HANGOUT
PAPERCUTZ

THE LOUD HOUSE
#9
"Ultimate Hangout"

nickelodeon
THE LOUD HOUSE
THE MANY FACES OF LINCOLN LOUD

THE LOUD HOUSE
#10
"The Many Faces of Lincoln Loud"

nickelodeon
THE LOUD HOUSE
WHO'S THE LOUDEST?

THE LOUD HOUSE
#11
"Who's the Loudest?"

nickelodeon
THE LOUD HOUSE
THE CASE OF THE STOLEN DRAWERS

THE LOUD HOUSE
#12
"The Case of the Stolen Drawers"

COMING SOON

nickelodeon
THE LOUD HOUSE
LUCY ROLLS THE DICE
PAPERCUTZ

THE LOUD HOUSE
#13
"Lucy Rolls the Dice"

nickelodeon
THE LOUD HOUSE
GUESSING GAMES
PAPERCUTZ

THE LOUD HOUSE
#14
"Guessing Games"

nickelodeon
THE LOUD HOUSE
THE MISSING LINC
PAPERCUTZ

THE LOUD HOUSE
#15
"The Missing Linc"

nickelodeon
THE LOUD HOUSE
LOUD AND CLEAR
PAPERCUTZ

THE LOUD HOUSE
#16
"Loud and Clear"

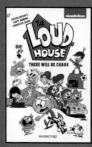

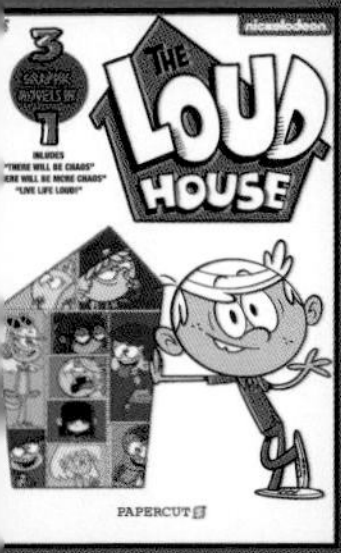
nickelodeon
THE LOUD HOUSE
PAPERCUTZ

THE LOUD HOUSE
3 IN 1
#1

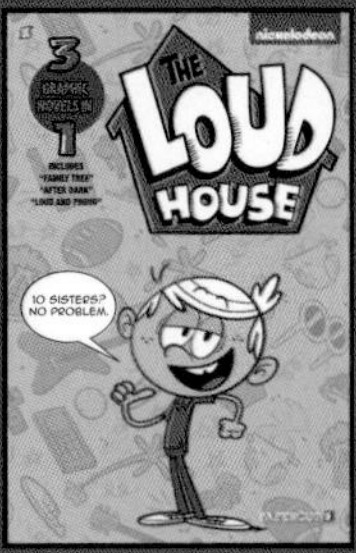
nickelodeon
THE LOUD HOUSE
10 SISTERS? NO PROBLEM.

THE LOUD HOUSE
3 IN 1
#2

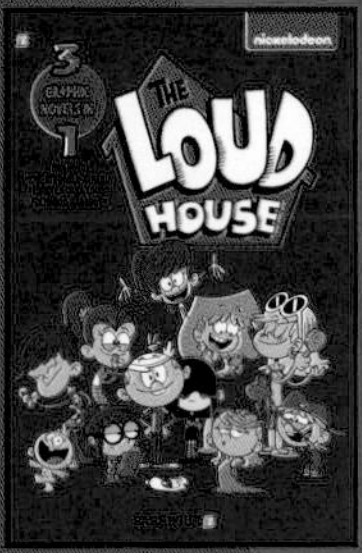
nickelodeon
THE LOUD HOUSE

THE LOUD HOUSE
3 IN 1
#3

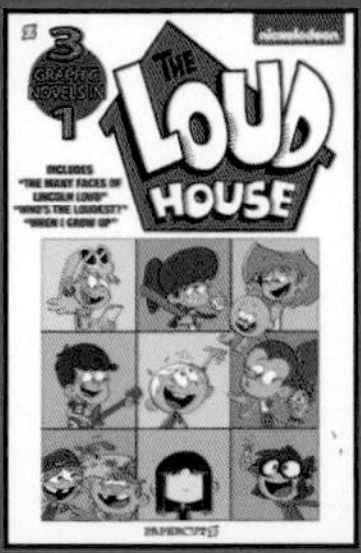
nickelodeon
THE LOUD HOUSE
PAPERCUTZ

THE LOUD HOUSE
3 IN 1
#4

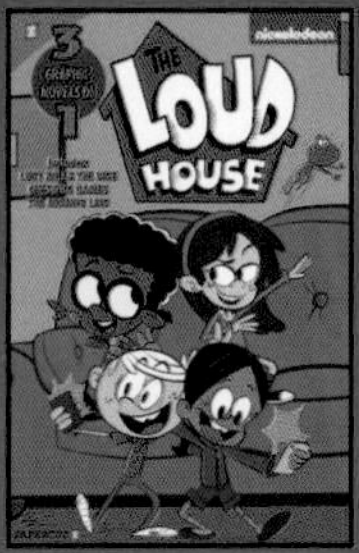
nickelodeon
THE LOUD HOUSE

THE LOUD HOUSE
3 IN 1
#5

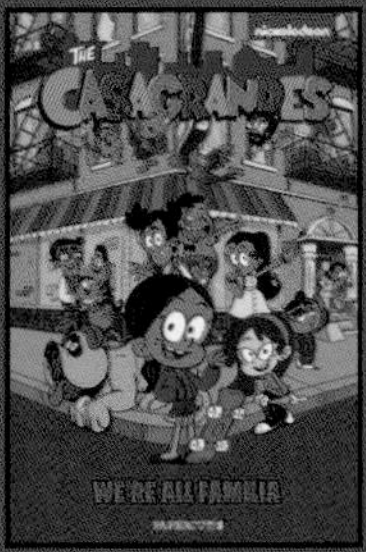
nickelodeon
THE CASAGRANDES
WE'RE ALL FAMILIA
PAPERCUTZ

THE CASAGRANDES
#1
"We're All Familia"

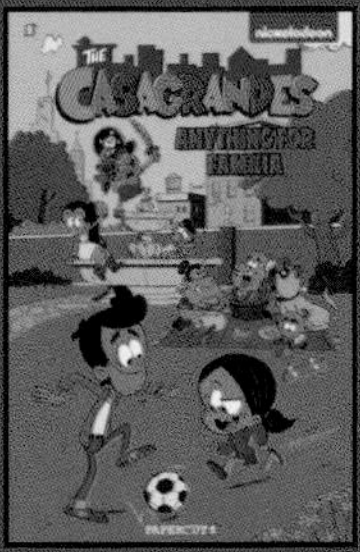
nickelodeon
THE CASAGRANDES
ANYTHING FOR FAMILIA

THE CASAGRANDES
#2
"Anything for Familia"

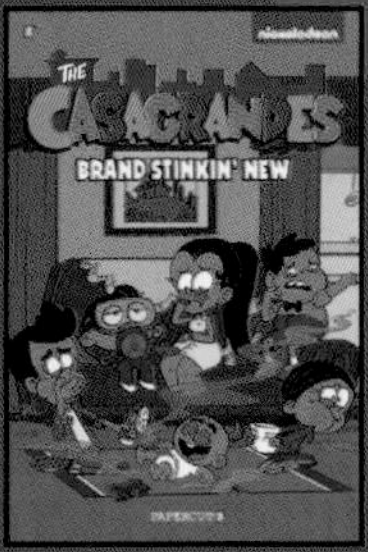
nickelodeon
THE CASAGRANDES
BRAND STINKIN' NEW
PAPERCUTZ

THE CASAGRANDES
#3
"Brand Stinkin' New"

COMING SOON

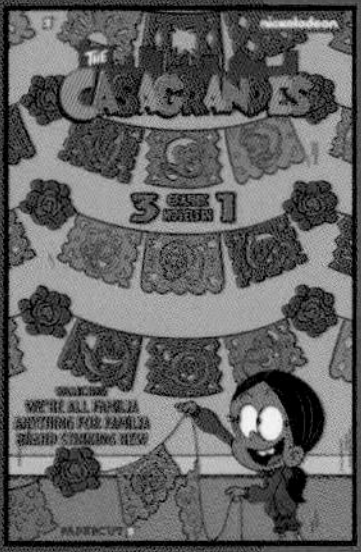
nickelodeon
THE CASAGRANDES

THE CASAGRANDES
3 IN 1
#1

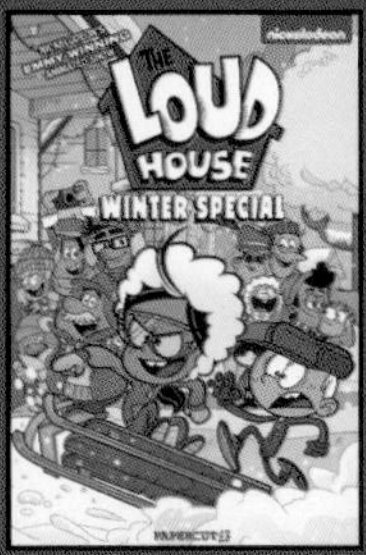
nickelodeon
THE LOUD HOUSE
WINTER SPECIAL
PAPERCUTZ

THE LOUD HOUSE
WINTER SPECIAL

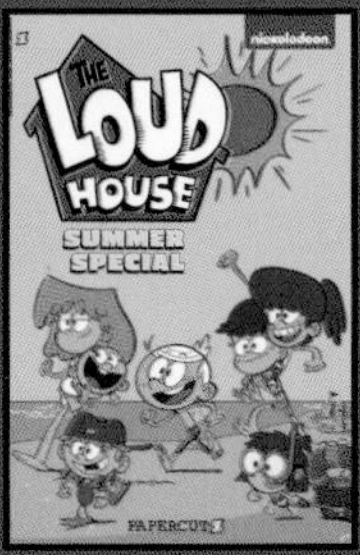
nickelodeon
THE LOUD HOUSE
SUMMER SPECIAL
PAPERCUTZ

THE LOUD HOUSE
SUMMER SPECIAL

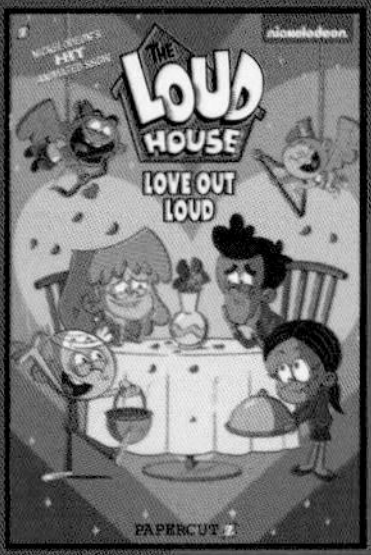
nickelodeon
THE LOUD HOUSE
LOVE OUT LOUD
PAPERCUTZ

THE LOUD HOUSE
LOVE OUT LOUD
SPECIAL

COMING SOON

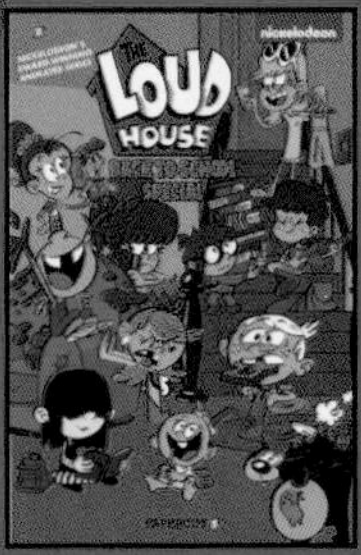
nickelodeon
THE LOUD HOUSE

THE LOUD HOUSE
BACK TO SCHOOL
SPECIAL

THE LOUD HOUSE and THE CASAGRANDES graphic novels and specials are available for $7.99 each in paperback, $12.99 each in hardcover. THE LOUD HOUSE 3 IN 1 and THE CASAGRANDES 3 IN 1 graphic novels are available for $14.99 each in paperback only.

Available from booksellers everywhere. You can also order online from Papercutz.com, or call 1-800-886-1223, Monday through Friday, 9-5 EST. MC, Visa, and AmEx accepted. To order by mail, please add $5.00 for postage and handling for the first book ordered, $1.00 for each additional book and make check payable to NBM Publishing. Send to: Papercutz, 160 Broadway, Suite 700, East Wing, New York, NY 10038.

The Loud House and Th **ligitally wherever**

WATCH OUT FOR PAPERCUTZ™

¡Hola! Welcome to the totally-new THE CASAGRANDES #3 "Brand Stinkin' New," from Papercutz, those multi-generational folks dedicated to publishing great graphic novels for all ages. I'm Jim Salicrup, the Editor-in-Chief and despite being "Brand Stinkin' Old," I can still connect with my inner child who sometimes seems a lot like Ronnie Anne's best bud, Lincoln Loud. Anyway, I'm here to make sure that you're aware of the other Nickelodeon graphic novels published by Papercutz, as well as to announce a couple of Papercutz personnel changes (Pretty exciting, eh?).

Of course, if you're a fan of both Papercutz and Nickelodeon—and who isn't?--you already know that Papercutz proudly publishes the on-going hit series, THE LOUD HOUSE, as well as offering up extra-special editions of THE LOUD HOUSE as well. As if that wasn't enough, those wonderful individual volumes of THE LOUD HOUSE graphic novels are also collected in THE LOUD HOUSE 3 IN I series, which collects 3 regular volumes of THE LOUD HOUSE in every volume. If you enjoy the adventures of Lincoln Loud, as well as his ten (count 'em!) sisters, Lori, Leni, Luna, Luan, Lynn, Lucy, Lola, Lana, Lisa, and Lily, Papercutz has made sure you have several ways to enjoy them in comics form— the regular series, the specials, and the 3 IN Is!

For fans of THE CASAGRANDES, this volume is special for a couple of reasons aside from featuring the Casagrandes in lots of enjoyable comic stories. First, being the third graphic novel of THE CASAGRANDES, that makes it possible for there to soon be the first (of many, we hope) THE CASAGRANDES 3 IN I! (Hmm, maybe we should call it *Tres en Uno*?) After all, we couldn't have published THE CASAGRANDES 3 IN I before we published three graphic novels of THE CASAGRANDES, right? This is great news if you're just joining us and were unable to find the first two graphic novels of THE CASAGRANDES.

But don't think we're just trying to sell you something! We always strongly suggest looking for THE CASAGRANDES (and every other Papercutz graphic novel) at your library. And if it's not immediately available at your library, they may be willing to put it on a pull list for you or even order it for you from another library! How great is that?

As for the second special thing about this third graphic novel of THE CASAGRANDES, it actually is all "Brand Stinkin' New"! While our first two volumes included a few stories originally published in THE LOUD HOUSE graphic novels, every story presented in this volume has never been published

anywhere else before. And that's going to continue in all THE CASAGRANDES graphic novels yet to come (well, except for the 3 IN I's, of course!).

Another hit series on Nickelodeon is THE SMURFS and Papercutz is smurfed to present THE SMURFS in multiple formats as well. THE SMURFS TALES brings you not only the Smurfs in their latest adventures, but other Smurftastic characters from Peyo, the creator of the Smurfs. Characters such as *Johan and Peewit* and *Benny Breakiron*. THE SMURFS 3 IN I series collects the earlier individual volumes of THE SMURFS that were published by Papercutz so you'll have plenty of Smurfs to enjoy!

For those of you who saw the *Watch Out for Papercutz* column in THE CASAGRANDES #2 you may recall we said good-bye (and wished her great success in all her future endeavors) to Joan Hilty, the multi-talented person who was the Nickelodeon Comics Editor ever since Papercutz started publishing Nickelodeon graphic novels. Now we must say good-bye to Papercutz Managing Editor Jeff Whitman, who after seven years at Papercutz, where he co-edited nearly everything with me and was the main editor on THE LOUD HOUSE and THE CASAGRANDES, he has decided to move on… to Nickelodeon!

That's right, Jeff is the new Comics Editor at Nickelodeon and we couldn't be happier for him. Stepping in to take over editing all THE LOUD HOUSE and THE CASAGRANDES graphic novels at Papercutz is erstwhile Papercutz Editorial Intern Karlo Antunes, and our new Assistant Managing Editor is Stephanie Brooks. While Joan Hilty may no longer be involved with our graphic novels, I'm thrilled that Jeff, Karlo, and Stephanie are. Everyone is super-excited and I suspect the very best is yet to come! Don't miss THE CASAGRANDES #4 "Friends and Family"—it's going to be *el mejor*!

Gracias,

Jim

STAY IN TOUCH!

EMAIL: salicrup@papercutz.com
WEB: papercutz.com
TWITTER: @papercutzgn
INSTAGRAM: @papercutzgn
FACEBOOK: PAPERCUTZGRAPHICNOVELS
FANMAIL: Papercutz, 160 Broadway, Suite 700, East Wing, New York, NY 10038

Go to papercutz.com and sign up for the free Papercutz e-newslette

Exclusive preview of THE LOUD HOUSE BACK TO SCHOOL SPECIAL

"SLEEPLESS IN PRESCHOOL"

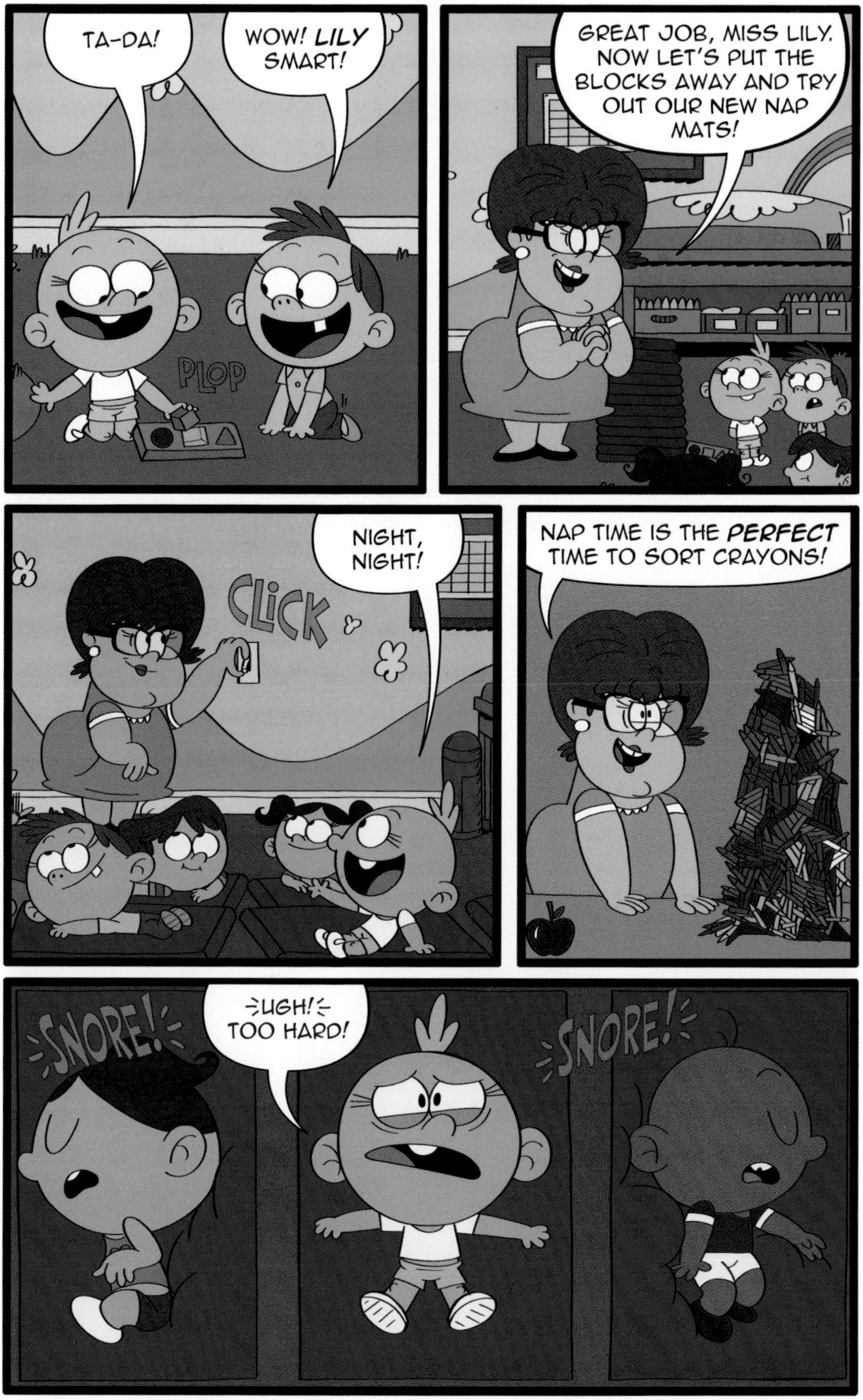

TA-DA!
WOW! LILY SMART!
PLOP
GREAT JOB, MISS LILY. NOW LET'S PUT THE BLOCKS AWAY AND TRY OUT OUR NEW NAP MATS!
CLICK
NIGHT, NIGHT!
NAP TIME IS THE PERFECT TIME TO SORT CRAYONS!
SNORE!
UGH! TOO HARD!
SNORE!

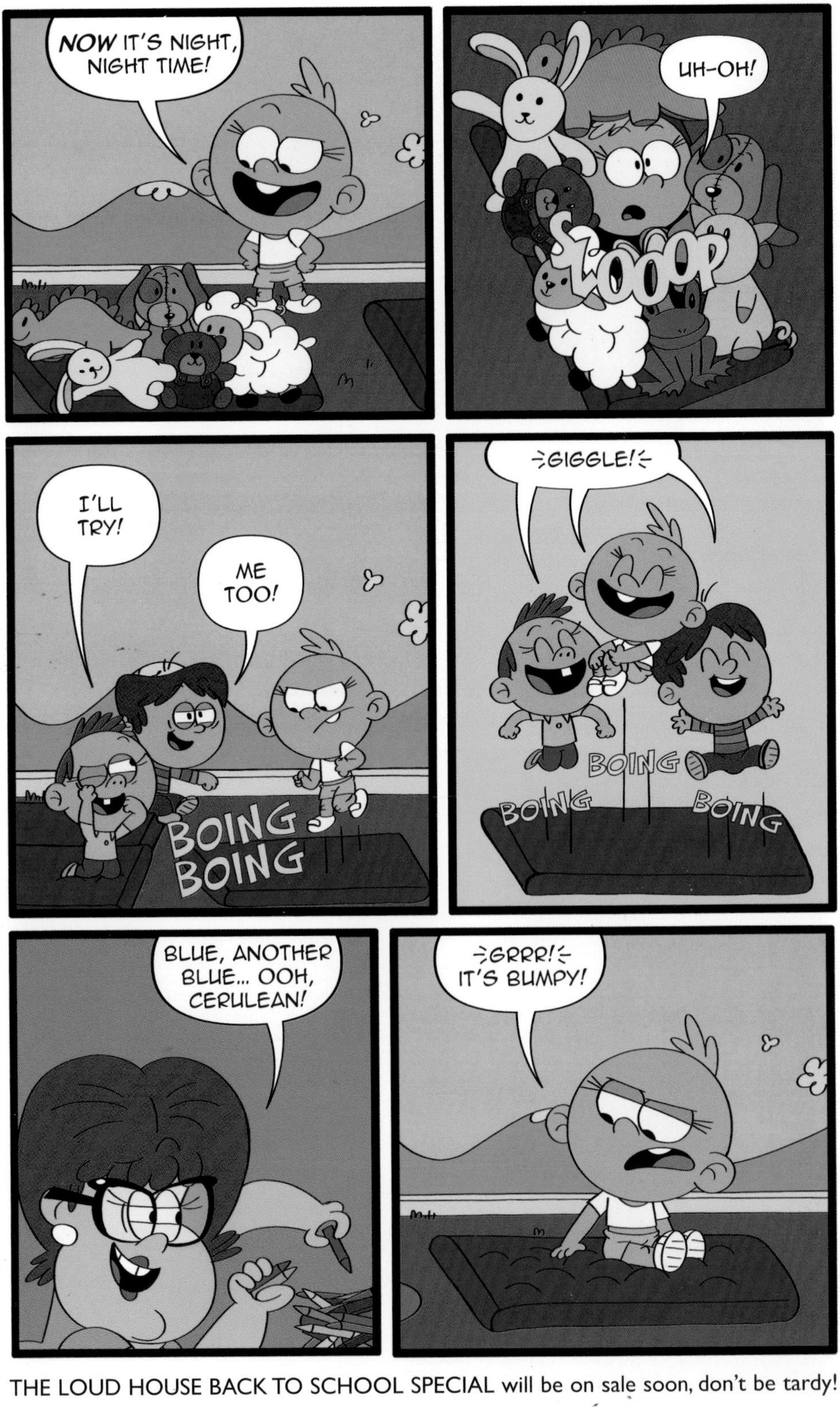
NOW IT'S NIGHT, NIGHT TIME!
UH-OH!
SZOOOP
I'LL TRY!
ME TOO!
BOING
BOING
GIGGLE!
BOING
BOING
BOING
BLUE, ANOTHER BLUE... OOH, CERULEAN!
GRRR! IT'S BUMPY!

THE LOUD HOUSE BACK TO SCHOOL SPECIAL will be on sale soon, don't be tardy!